Walt Disney's
Bambi

Senior Designer: Elaine Lopez
Editor: Sharon Yates
Editorial Director: Pamela Pia

Walt Disney's Bambi copyright © 1941, 2001, 2004 Disney Enterprises, Inc.
From the story by Felix Salten. Illustrations adapted by Melvin Shaw.

C E

Copyright ©2008 Disney Enterprises, Inc. All Rights Reserved.
Published by Reader's Digest Children's Books,
Reader's Digest Road, Pleasantville, NY U.S.A. 10570-7000
and Reader's Digest Children's Publishing Limited,
The Ice House, 124-126 Walcot Street, Bath UK BA1 5BG
Reader's Digest Children's Books, the Pegasus logo,
and Reader's Digest are all registered trademarks of
The Reader's Digest Association, Inc. Manufactured in China.
1 3 5 7 9 10 8 6 4 2

Walt Disney's
Bambi

Illustrations by The Walt Disney Studios

From the story by Felix Salten
Illustrations adapted by Melvin Shaw

Reader's Digest
Children's Books™

Pleasantville, New York • Montréal, Québec • Bath, United Kingdom

When Bambi was born, the forest animals came to greet him.

$\mathcal{B}$ambi came into the world in the middle of a forest thicket. The little, hidden thicket was scarcely big enough for the new baby and his mother.

But a magpie soon spied him there.

"What a beautiful baby!" she cried. And away she flew to spread the news to all the other animals of the forest.

Her chattering soon brought dozens of birds and animals to the thicket. The rabbits came hurrying; the squirrels came a-scurrying. The robins and bluebirds fluttered and flew.

At last, even the old owl woke up from his long day's sleep.

"Who, who?" the owl said sleepily, hearing all the commotion.

"Wake up, Friend Owl!" a rabbit called. "It's happened! The young prince is born!"

"Everyone's going to see him," said the squirrels. "You must come, too."

With a sigh, the owl spread his wings and flew off toward the thicket. There he found squirrels and rabbits and birds peering through the bushes at a doe and a little spotted fawn.

The fawn was Bambi, the new Prince of the Forest.

"Congratulations," said the owl, speaking for all the animals. "This is quite an occasion. It isn't often that a prince is born in the forest."

The doe looked up. "Thank you," she said quietly. Then with her nose she gently nudged her sleeping baby until he lifted his head and looked around.

She nudged him again, and licked him reassuringly. At last, he pushed up on his thin legs, trying to stand.

"Look! He's trying to stand up already!" shouted one of the little rabbits, named Thumper. "He's awfully wobbly, though, isn't he?"

Thumper, the bunny, became Bambi's first friend.

"Thumper!" the mother rabbit exclaimed, pulling him back. "That's not a pleasant thing to say!"

The new fawn's legs were not very steady, it was true, but at last he stood beside his mother. Now, all the animals could see the fine white spots on his red-brown coat, and the sleepy expression on his soft baby face.

The forest around him echoed with countless small voices. A soft breeze rustled the leaves about the thicket. And the watching animals whispered among themselves. But the little fawn did not listen to any of them. He only knew that his mother's tongue was licking him softly, washing and warming him. He nestled closer to her, and closed his sleepy eyes.

Bambi learned to play games with the bunnies.

Quietly, the animals and birds slipped away through the forest.

Thumper, the rabbit, was the last to go.

"What are you going to name the young prince?" he asked.

"I'll call him Bambi," the mother answered.

"Bambi," Thumper said. "Bambi. That's a good name. Good-bye, Bambi." And he hopped away after his sisters.

Bambi was not a sleepy baby for long. Soon he was following his mother down the narrow forest paths. Bright flowers winked at him from beneath the leaves. Prickly branches tickled his legs as he passed.

Squirrels and chipmunks looked up and called, "Good morning, young prince."

Opossums, hanging by their long tails from a tree branch, said, "Hello, Prince Bambi."

The fawn looked at them all with wondering eyes. But he did not say a word.

Finally, as Bambi and his mother reached a little clearing in the forest, they met Thumper and his family.

"Hi, Bambi," said Thumper. "Come on and play."

"Yes, let's play!" Thumper's sisters cried. And away they hopped, over branches and hillocks and tufts of grass.

Bambi soon understood the game, and he began to jump and run on his stiff, spindly legs.

Thumper jumped over a log and his sisters followed.

"Come on, Bambi," Thumper called. "Hop over the log."

Bambi jumped, but not far enough. He fell with a plop on top of the log.

"Too bad," said Thumper. "You'll do better next time."

Bambi untangled his legs and stood up again. But still he did not speak. He pranced along behind Thumper, and soon he saw a family of birds sitting on a branch.

Bambi looked at them.

"Those are birds, Bambi," Thumper told him. "Birds."

"Bir-d," Bambi said slowly. The young prince had spoken his first word!

Thumper and his sisters were all excited, and Bambi was pleased, too. He repeated the word over and over to himself.

Then he saw a butterfly cross the path. "Bird, bird!" he cried again.

"No, Bambi," said Thumper. "That's not a bird. That's a butterfly."

The butterfly disappeared into a clump of yellow flowers. Bambi bounded toward them happily.

"Butterfly!" he cried.

"No, Bambi," said Thumper. "Not butterfly. *Flower*."

Thumper pushed his nose into the flowers and sniffed. Bambi did the same, but suddenly he drew back. His nose had touched something warm and furry.

Out from the bed of flowers came a small black and white head with two shining eyes.

"Flower!" cried Bambi.

As the little animal stepped out, the white stripe down his black furry back glistened in the sun.

Thumper was laughing so hard that he could barely speak.

"That's not a flower," said Thumper. "That's a skunk."

"Flower," Bambi said again.

"I don't care," said the skunk. "The young prince can call me Flower if he wants to. I don't mind."

And that's how Flower, the skunk, got his name.

Bambi and his friends would play together in the spring.

One morning, Bambi and his mother walked down a new path. It grew lighter and lighter as they walked along. Soon the trail ended in a tangle of bushes and vines, and Bambi could see a great, bright, open space spread out before them.

Bambi wanted to bound out there to play in the sunshine, but his mother stopped him. "Wait," she said. "You must never run out on the meadow without first making sure it is safe."

She took a few slow, careful steps forward. She listened and sniffed in all directions. Then she called, "Come."

Bambi ran out. He felt so good and so happy that he leaped into the air again and again. For the meadow was the most beautiful place he had ever seen.

His mother dashed forward and showed him how to race and play in the tall grass. Bambi ran after her. He felt as if he were flying. Round and round they raced in great circles. At last, his mother stopped and stood still, catching her breath.

Bambi saw his own face in a meadow pool.

Then Bambi and his mother set out to explore the meadow. Soon he spied his little friend the skunk, sitting in the shade of some blossoms.

"Good morning, Flower," said Bambi.

Next he found Thumper and his sisters nibbling on some sweet clover.

"Try some, Bambi," said Thumper.

So Bambi did.

Suddenly, a big green frog popped out of the clover patch and hopped over to a meadow pond. Bambi had not seen the pond before, so he hurried over for a closer look.

As the fawn came near, the frog hopped into the water.

Where could he have gone? Bambi wondered. So he bent down to look into the pond. As the ripples cleared, Bambi jumped back. For he saw a fawn down there in the water, looking up at him!

"Don't be frightened, Bambi," his mother said to him. "You are just seeing yourself in the water."

Bambi met another little fawn. Her name was Faline.

So Bambi looked once more. This time he saw *two* fawns looking out at him! He jumped back again, and as he lifted his head, he saw that it was true — there was another little fawn standing beside him!

"Hello," she said.

Bambi backed away and ran to his mother, where she was quietly eating grass beside another doe. Bambi leaned against her and peered out at the other little fawn, who had followed him there.

"Don't be afraid, Bambi," his mother said. "This is little Faline, and this is your Aunt Ena. Can't you say hello to them?"

"Hello, Bambi," said the two deer. But Bambi did not say a word.

"You have been wanting to meet other deer," his mother reminded him. "Well, Aunt Ena and Faline are deer just like us. Now, can't you speak to them?"

"Hello," whispered Bambi in a small, small voice.

"Come and play, Bambi," said Faline. She leaned forward and licked his face.

Bambi dashed away as fast as he could run, and Faline raced after him. They almost flew over the meadow.

Up and down they chased each other. Over the little hillocks they raced.

When they stopped, all topsy-turvy and breathless, they were good friends.

Then they walked side by side on the bright meadow, visiting quietly together.

One day, Bambi awoke to find the world white with snow.

Thumper took a run and slid swiftly across the pond. Bambi tried it, too, but his legs shot out from under him and down he crashed onto the hard ice. That was not so much fun.

"Let's play something else," Bambi suggested, when he had carefully pulled himself to his feet again. "Where's Flower?"

"I think I know," said Thumper.

He led Bambi to the doorway of a deep burrow. They peered down into it. There, peacefully sleeping on a bed of withered flowers, lay the little skunk.

"Wake up, Flower!" Bambi called.

"Is it spring yet?" Flower asked sleepily, half opening his eyes.

"No, winter's just beginning," Bambi said. "What are you doing?"

"Hibernating," the little skunk replied. "Flowers like to sleep in the winter, you know."

Thumper yawned. "I guess I'll take a nap, too," he said. "Good-bye, Bambi. I'll see you later."

So Bambi was left alone. Sadly, he wandered back to the thicket.

"Don't fret, Bambi," his mother said. "Winter will soon be over, and spring will come again."

So Bambi went to sleep beside his mother in the snug, warm thicket, and dreamed of the jolly games that he and his friends would play when springtime came again.